Clifford's Fairy Tails

THE THREE LITTLE PIGS AND THE BIG RED DOG

CLIFFORD CREATED BY NORMAN BRIDWELL

WRITTEN BY DAPHNE PENDERGRASS AND ILLUSTRATED BY RÉMY SIMARD

SCHOLASTIC INC.

Scholastic and The Norman Bridwell Trust have worked with a carefully selected author and illustrator
to ensure that this book is of the same quality as the original Clifford book series.

10 9 8 7 6 5 4 3 2   18 19 20 21 22
ISBN 978-1-338-20235-9 • Printed in the U.S.A. 40 • First printing 2018 • Book design by Erin McMahon

Hello, I'm Emily Elizabeth, and this is Clifford, my big red dog. Every night, we cuddle up and my dad tells us a story.

My dad loves making Clifford and me the stars of the story.
Tonight we're reading *The Three Little Pigs and the Big Bad Wolf*.

Once upon a time,
Clifford and his best friend,
Emily Elizabeth, moved
to a new village. They
were excited to meet their
neighbors, the three little
pigs. They had even baked
a pie for each pig.

Just as they were
about to leave, Clifford
let out a horrible
sneeze.

Clifford's sneeze rattled the whole house!
"Clifford!" Emily Elizabeth cried. "You're
sick. You should stay home and rest."
But Clifford wouldn't stay. He wanted to
meet his new neighbors!

Emily Elizabeth and Clifford arrived at the first
little pig's house. His house was made of straw.

"By the hair of my chinny-chin-chin, it's my new neighbors!" said the first little pig.

Just then, Clifford felt another sneeze coming on. He huffed, and he puffed, until . . .

. . . he blew the straw house down!

Clifford and Emily Elizabeth apologized. Then they helped the little pig out from under the mess.

The little pig gave Clifford a big blanket to use as a hanky. "You should really go home and get some rest," he said.

Clifford wouldn't go home—he had to meet his other two neighbors and deliver the pies. And he wanted to help fix the first little pig's house, too!

So Clifford, Emily Elizabeth, and the first little pig walked to the next pig's house. This pig's house was made out of sticks.

"By the hair of my chinny-chin-chin, it's my new neighbors, and my brother, too!" said the second little pig.

Just then, Clifford felt a sneeze coming on. He huffed, and he puffed, until . . .

. . . he blew the
stick house down.

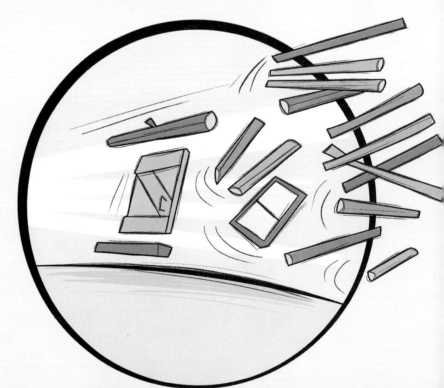

"You should really cover your snout when you sneeze," the second little pig grunted.

"Clifford, your sneezes are getting worse," said Emily Elizabeth. "Let's get you home."

But Clifford refused. He wanted to meet his neighbors, he hadn't given the pigs their pies, and now he had *two* houses to help rebuild!

So Clifford, Emily Elizabeth, and the two little pigs walked to the next pig's house. His house was made out of bricks.

"By the hair of my chinny-chin-chin, it's my new neighbors, and my brothers, too!" said the third little pig.

Just then, Clifford felt a sneeze coming on. He tried to cover his nose, but it was no use.

The sneeze couldn't be stopped! He huffed, and he puffed . . .

This was Clifford's biggest sneeze yet!

But the brick house *didn't* fall down!
"You've got a nasty cold!" said the third little pig.
"You better come inside and rest."

The third little pig made a big pot of soup for Clifford. He also wrapped him in as many blankets as he could find.

While Clifford rested, Emily Elizabeth gave each pig a pie. After a while, Clifford was feeling much better.

Later, the third little pig gathered bricks and building supplies to help his brothers fix their houses.

Clifford and Emily Elizabeth helped, too.

Just as they were almost finished, Clifford started to huff and puff . . .

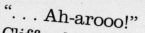

"... Ah-arooo!"

Clifford barked happily. He was feeling back to normal, and he was happy to help his new friends.

And the three little pigs? They were happy, too. Now they had houses Clifford could never sneeze down!

AH-AROOO!!!!

THE END